Chiara Valentina Segré
Paolo Domeniconi

Oscar
the Guardian Cat

GIBBS SMITH
TO ENRICH AND INSPIRE HUMANKIND

My name is Oscar and I am a cat. But mind you, I'm not one of those furballs that just sleeps and eats. It's not that I don't like a big bowl of cat food, but I'm not a cat like other cats. I am a guardian cat.

Regular cats live in regular homes; Hope House, where I live, has seventy-three bedrooms and a big park with a long hedge where I go to hunt blackbirds.

There are no children in Hope House, but there are seventy-three grandmas and grandpas, plus nurses, doctors, cooks, and gardeners who come in every day.

A guardian cat is never bored in Hope House. Every morning I check to make sure that everyone is awake. I check under the beds and I chew on the flower blossoms (except for the ones with thorns; once I bit a cactus and I had to eat chicken broth for a week).

In the afternoon I take a nap in the park's flower beds. In the evening I am busy in the dining hall. Grandmas and grandpas are like children. They spill and drop food on the floor. That means snack time for me!

But I have to watch out for Dolores, the head nurse. She gets upset if anyone has a dirty uniform or scratches the couch in the visitor's room. Even Dr. Bonner, who is more than two feet taller than her, is afraid of her scolding.

Dolores is like a cat: a little surly, but good and kindhearted. That's why I like her. Even though when I see her in the dining hall, I have to run away quickly. Otherwise I'm in trouble!

The grandmas and grandpas at Hope House are not always the same ones. Some stay for such a short time that I don't get a chance to become familiar with their smell. Others have always been here, as far as a cat can remember.

Ms. Lisa sleeps in room 307.

Ms. Lisa can't talk anymore and she is always quiet, even when her grandchildren come to visit. But she smiles when they bring her flowers.

Maybe Ms. Lisa just speaks with smiles instead of words. She talks to me a lot, because she always smiles when she sees me.

On the other hand, Mr. Olsen in room 212 talks a lot; the only problem is that Dolores and Dr. Bonner don't understand him because he often mixes up his words.

When that happens, Mr. Olsen hits his head and cries. Then I jump on his lap to soothe him so Dolores can put him back to bed.

Words really aren't that important in Hope House after all.

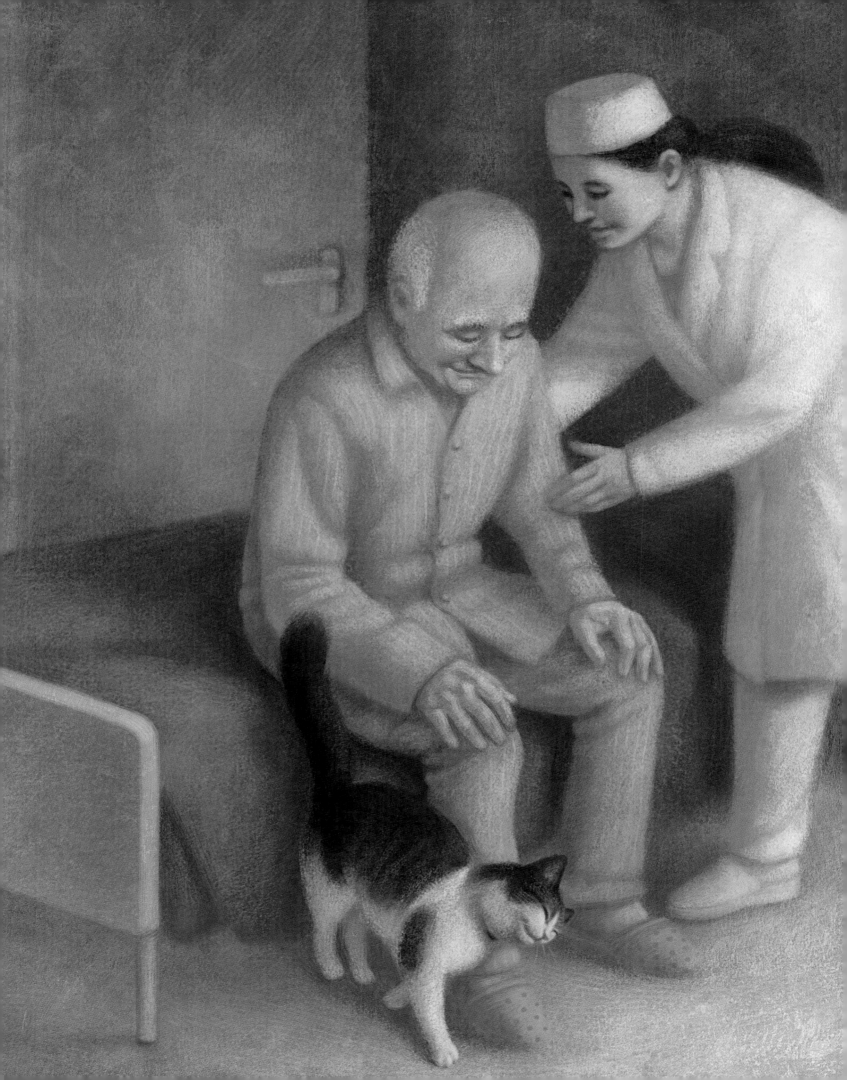

Life is good at Hope House, even if it's a little crazy sometimes. One night there was a thunderstorm that rattled the windows. I calmly sat in the visitor's room, cleaning my paws.

All of a sudden there was a commotion. Dolores ran back and forth with her hair flying out from under her cap. Since the nurses run around like crazy at least three times a week, I patiently sat there cleaning my fur.

When I saw Dr. Bonner go by with his glasses perched on his nose, I understood that something serious was happening. I stretched and went to check it out. After all, I am the guardian cat.

When I got to room 212, I understood: Mr. Olsen wasn't in bed. I ran up and down the stairs, peeked in the medicine cabinet, and looked under the table in the dining hall; Mr. Olsen wasn't anywhere (and he *is* pretty big and tall).

We found him in the basement, in his bare feet on the freezing floor. "Helllllpppp, bombs!" he yelled each time there was a clap of thunder.

"Joey, I'll protect you." Joey is Mr. Olsen's younger brother, but he has a white beard now and certainly wasn't in the basement in Hope House; Mr. Olsen was talking to a fire extinguisher. This was a job for the guardian cat.

With my tail straight and my nose in the air, I produced one of my best "Meows." Mr. Olsen whispered to the extinguisher, "We're safe, Joey. Oscar found us."

So holding on to my tail, Mr. Olsen went back to bed to warm up his freezing feet. With one hand he cradled the fire extinguisher as if it were a kitten.

"Thanks, Oscar. Can you stay with him a while?" asked Dr. Bonner, but I was already on my way out.

"Oscar only stays for special moments," said Dolores, putting another cover over Mr. Olsen's feet, who was sleeping with the fire extinguisher in his arms.

The next afternoon, while Mr. Olsen was in the park, Dolores put the fire extinguisher back in the basement. I don't think he noticed, because he gets distracted and forgets things.

Mrs. Olsen and her daughter have to introduce themselves every time they come to visit. But he has never forgotten my name: Oscar.

After the storm, the days passed quietly at Hope House. Then last night something special happened.

It was a guardian cat night.

I was doing the nighttime rounds with Dolores. Someone was waiting for us in the farthest and darkest corner of room 212. It was Mewt.

Humans are really strange. They find a cat's hair in a bowl of soup (and when that happens, it's better if I run away from Dolores), but they never notice Mewt is there.

She's pretty big, certainly more than a cat like me. Mewt comes to Hope House often. A lot of people call her and ask her to come quickly. But she doesn't come when asked. She only comes at the right time.

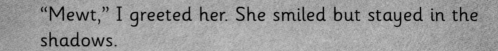

"Mewt," I greeted her. She smiled but stayed in the shadows.

When Mewt comes to see someone, that means I need to stay. Dolores or Dr. Bonner can't do it because they have to look after the other grandmas and grandpas at Hope House. And as I mentioned, they don't see Mewt.

So it's me, Oscar, who stays. I'm the guardian cat.

I jumped on the bed, circled around to find the best spot, and then curled up on Mr. Olsen's chest, purring.

Dolores pushed the medicine cart down the hallway. When she saw me on the bed through the half-closed door, she left the cart in the hallway and went to look for Mrs. Olsen's phone number.

Meanwhile, nestled with Mr. Olsen's gentle breathing, I continued to purr. I wasn't sleeping; I was looking at Mewt.

That evening she had long blonde hair and big blue eyes. She looked just like the little girl whose hand Mr. Olsen was holding in the photo that Mrs. Olsen had put on his nightstand.

Last week, when Mewt had come for Ms. Lisa, she had curly black hair like her grandson who always brought her a rose.

Ms. Lisa had smiled at Mewt too.

"Mewt," I called a second time, but she didn't move. It wasn't time yet.

Mr. Olsen was watching her too. His eyes were open and he looked afraid. I knew that Mewt was good and only ever came at the right time, but Mr. Olsen didn't recognize her.

I was there to tell Mr. Olsen not to be afraid.

When the last sliver of the sun dipped behind the hills, I called her a third time: "Mewt."

Finally Mewt left the dark corner and walked over to the bed. Mr. Olsen wasn't afraid anymore because I was at his side, and when a cat purrs it's hard not to trust it.

Mewt took Mr. Olsen's hand, the same one he had laid on me. I purred even more. At her touch, Mr. Olsen's eyes were no longer a deep black pool but bright and alive like in the photo on the nightstand.

Now Mr. Olsen laughed. Mewt's hand, golden in the light of dusk, was warm and soft like a cat's fur. Finally Mr. Olsen closed his eyes with a smile, dreaming of running in a field with a little blonde girl with blue eyes.

Then, hand in hand, Mewt and Mr. Olsen got up from the bed and flew out the window toward the sunset. When I turned my head they had disappeared, just like every other time.

But I didn't move. I'm Oscar the guardian cat. I stay when Mewt arrives and I wait until morning.

The sun had just come up when Mrs. Olsen arrived with her daughter, with the same blue eyes as in the photo but a little more sad.

There was no trace of Mewt; only me, Oscar, and I slept blissfully.

Now that Mr. Olsen was with his family, I got up, stretched my back, yawning a big cat yawn with my tail straight and proud, and went out the door.

I don't know when I'll see Mewt again, but it's another day at Hope House.

I'm Oscar the guardian cat and I have a lot of things to do. I have to visit seventy-two rooms, chase the blackbirds in the park, and today make sure no one has moved Joey . . . sorry . . . Mr. Olsen's fire extinguisher from the basement.

A guardian cat is never bored in Hope House.

This book is inspired by the true story of Oscar the cat, who lives in the Steere House Nursing & Rehabilitation Center in Providence, Rhode Island, and accompanies patients on their most important journey.

First published in Italy
Original title: *Oscar il gatto custode*
Copyright © 2015 Camelozampa, Italy

Published in the United States of America by
Gibbs Smith
P.O. Box 667
Layton, Utah 84041
Copyright © 2018 Camelozampa, Italy

Manufactured in December 2017 in China by Crash Paper Co.

First Edition
22 21 20 19 18   5 4 3 2 1

1.800.835.4993 orders
www.gibbs-smith.com

Gibbs Smith books are printed on either recycled, 100% post-consumer waste, FSC-certified papers or on paper produced from sustainable PEFC-certified forest/controlled wood source. Learn more at www.pefc.org.

Library of Congress Control Number: 2017950752
ISBN: 978-1-4236-4934-2